Which is WITCH?

WINNIE
on Patrol

WINNIE'S
Fun Run

Crash! Winnie flung open the door and threw her shopping down.

'Wilbur, where are you? Wilburrrr?'

Wilbur was lying in a nice hot patch of sunshine on the floor behind the worm-noodle machine. He opened one eye, then closed it again.

'Wiiiiiillllbuuurrrr!' yelled Winnie.

Wilbur yawned a wide yawn. He stretched a wide stretch. Then he sighed.

'Wilbur!' Winnie pounced, grabbing

him and clutching him to her chest.
'Guess what, Wilbur?'

Wilbur raised an eyebrow.

'There's a fun run this afternoon, and
it's fancy dress! With prizes!! Ooo, what
shall I be, Wilbur? Something lovely-
dovely beautiful-fruitiful!'

Wilbur rolled his eyes.

'*Abracadabra!*' went Winnie, and
in an instant, there she was, dressed
as a mermaid.

8

'I'll just get my comb from the dressing-up table,' said Winnie.

But mermaids can't walk very well. They are even worse at running.

Wobble-splat-crash!

'Blooming bloomers!' said Winnie, rubbing her elbow. 'I need a fancy dress outfit for somebody who uses legs a lot. I know! *Abracadabra!*'

9

Instantly, Winnie became a ballerina,
twirling and swirling and twiddling and
twaddling on her tippy-toe tootsies
until ... **Crash!**

'Heck in a handbag!' said Winnie, rubbing her leg. 'That's no flipping good either!'

Wilbur put a claw to his chin and thought. Then he raised his claw in the air. 'Meeow!'

'What, Wilbur? What should I dress up as?'

Wilbur pointed to a picture on a wall of a handsome knight and a princess.

'That's it!' said Winnie. *'Abracadabra!'*

And there stood Winnie in a suit of armour. **Clang! Wobble-clash crash!**

'Ouch!' said Winnie, rubbing her head. 'Er . . . or did you mean the girl one, Wilbur?'

'Meeeow!'

12

'Abracadabra!' Instantly Winnie was dressed as a princess. Frills and flounces, bows and bouncy bits, and all-over-pink.

'Oooo. I think I like this one!' said Winnie. 'I'll be the prettiest one there, don't you think, Wilbur?'

'Mmm,' said Wilbur.

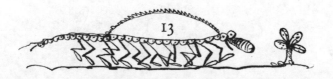

'I'll win that big cup for the best costume, easy-peasy, elephant-with-a-cold sneezy! And I might even win the race cup too. Then I could put one at each end of the mantelpiece. I wonder if I can run in this dress?'

Winnie took a tentative step. Then another. She did a little jig. Then she ran around the room.

'This is brillaramaroodles for running in, but I must make sure I've got enough energy to run faster than everyone else. I need an energy drink.'

Winnie found a bottle of pond water and added some gnat's-pee cordial. 'But there's not much energy in those. Perhaps I can have some energy-boosting food.

Oo, I know what'll make me go fast!'
Winnie took down a jar from a top shelf.
She mixed cheetah claw clippings with
rocket-engine oil and ground them up to
make a smelly paste. Winnie held her
nose, and gulped down a big spoonful.

'Yuerk!' she said. 'Ooo, that is so very very very disgusting it must make a big difference!' And within moments it did make a difference. It made Winnie go very fast . . . to the loo!

When Winnie came out of the loo, she didn't look fit to run anywhere.

'I'm weak and wobbly!' wailed Winnie. 'Wilbur, however am I going to race?'

Wilbur helped Winnie down to the fun run field. Winnie tried warming up, running on the spot, knees hitting her chin, just for a moment. Then she collapsed and gasped for breath. 'Ooo, Wilbur, I'm as panty as a knicker factory! I can't run!' Then Winnie suddenly smiled. 'What if I had some trainers that would do the running for me? Am I a genius, Wilbur, or what?'

'Mrrrow,' said Wilbur.

'Abradacabra!' went Winnie, pointing her princessy pink wand at her princess shoes, and—zap!

18

Instantly her shoes turned into super
sporty speedy spongy sleeky stylish
trainers.

'On your marks!' said the race starter.
'Get set . . . GO!' And off ran everyone in
their costumes, all together . . . except for
Winnie, who was way out in front.

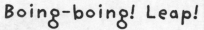

Boing-boing! Leap!

'Wow!' shouted Winnie. 'These are seven-league trainers! Watch me go!'

But Winnie's new trainers had a mind of their own. They veered Winnie off the track. They ran her dashing through hedges. Splashing through ditches. Thrashing through a haystack.

'Meeow!' called Wilbur as Winnie
shrank into the distance. The left trainer
must have been slightly stronger than the
right one because Winnie was going round
in a great big circle. Wilbur scratched his
head, then, 'Mrroww!' he said. He had a
plan. Wilbur found Jerry in the crowd,
and he dragged him to stand with his
arms out.

'Meeow, mrrrrrrow!' Wilbur told
Scruff, so then Scruff knew what to do.
Then they waited.

21

Meanwhile, Winnie was charging through the vegetable market. **Bang! Tumble! Squash! Splat!**

'Help!' **Pant pant!**

Winnie ran through the clothes market. **Rip! Tangle! Whoops! Sob, pant pant!**

But Winnie's trainers were running and running . . . back to where the race began. And there was Jerry with his arms out.

Oomph! Winnie ran slap bang into Jerry. Winnie's trainers were still running, but Jerry lifted Winnie off the ground. And then Scruff and Wilbur tackled a trainer each.

'Grrrr!'

'Hisss!'

22

They tugged and tussled those trainers
off Winnie's feet, and they spat them out.
Pah! Off ran the trainers, all on their own.
They are probably running still.

So Winnie could wibbly-wobbly stand
on her feet again, and not go anywhere.

'Oooo, I'm as shaky as a slug slime
jelly. I never want to take another step!'
she said. 'Fetch me a pushchair, would
you?'

The fun runners were arriving back, and the winners were being announced by a crackly voice coming out of a loudspeaker. 'The winner of the best fancy dress costume is Winnie the Witch for her very convincing outfit and make-up!'

'Hooray!' shouted the crowd.

'Oh!' Winnie patted her hair. 'Well, I'm as surprised as a hair louse that wins a best pet award! Come with me to fetch the cup, Wilbur!'

Wilbur helped Winnie wobble up onto the stage to collect a huge twiddly trophy.

'There you are, madam,' said the man. 'Well deserved for your very impressive scarecrow outfit.'

'Scare—!' began an affronted Winnie.
But Wilbur put a quick paw over her
mouth and dragged her off the stage.

'Ah, well,' said Winnie as Jerry gave her
a piggyback home. 'I'd rather be an
impressive scarecrow than just one of a
herd of pink princesses.'

'Meow,' agreed Wilbur.

WINNIE
Gets Bossy

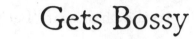

Winnie sat with her dirty boots up on the fat-bellied armchair, spilling pop-corns and pop-bunions as she sat watching the telly.

Scratch-tug-tattify! Wilbur was happily scratching down the side of the same chair. His claws were ripping the fabric and tugging out the stuffing.

'See this?' said Winnie. 'That man's showing how you can make your room look interesting and new, just by moving

your furniture about a bit. Let's try it!'

Up jumped Winnie, spilling her fizzy pickle-pop onto the chair seat. 'Let's move the big table over to the window,' said Winnie. Winnie pushed. 'Phew! Come on, Wilbur, lend us a paw!'

So Wilbur pushed too. The table dug its heels in.

Scrape-screech! Puff-pant!
went Winnie and Wilbur. The table was
leaving lines of scrape marks.

'Oh, flipping fish flippers, look at that!'
said Winnie. 'Pass me that rug, Wilbur.'

Wilbur and Winnie put the rug over the

marks, but, **trip-smash!**

31

'That blooming rug tripped me on purpose!' said Winnie. 'Humph!' Winnie pulled out her wand. 'If all you pieces of furniture think that you can behave as if you're alive, then you might as well be alive and blooming well move yourselves! Most of you have got legs, so you can just walk to where I want you!'

Winnie waved her wand.

'Abracadabra!'

Instantly the furniture sat up straight.

'Ooo, that's better!' said Winnie. 'Right then, chairs, tuck in around the table. Go!'

Hup-two-three, the dining chairs marched smartly into place, neatly under the table.

'Brillaramaroodles!' said Winnie.
'Where's the elephant's earwax polish?'
Winnie put the tin of polish and one of her
old vests onto the table. 'Polish yourself,
please, table!' she said.

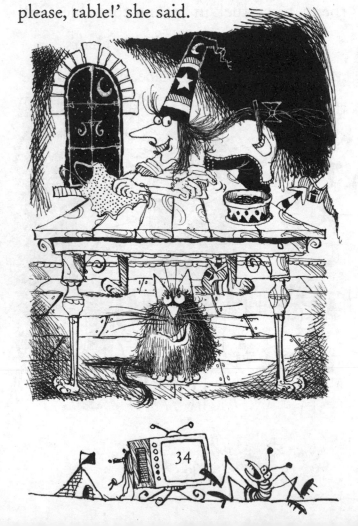

Up came one of the table's four legs to take hold of the polish tin. Up came another leg to take hold of the cloth. Then the table polished itself like a person brushing their hair.

'Oo, what else shall we make the furniture do?' said Winnie.

She went from room to room.

'Bed, make yourself!'

Winnie's bed did a kind of a jiggle and quiver, and all the bed covers fell into place, all neat and tight.

'Curtains, draw yourselves!'

Swish-swoosh!

'Ha haa! Do it again!' said Winnie.

Swish-swoosh!

'This is fun!'

Back downstairs, Winnie ordered,

'Chairs, do an Irish dance!'

The chairs shuffled out from under the table. They all lined up in a straight row. Their arms went down by their sides, then their legs began to prance and dance on the spot.

'Yay!' cheered Winnie. She and Wilbur joined in the dance. 'Hatstand, do a disco dance!'

And it did.

'Ha haa!' laughed Winnie. 'What next?'

Wilbur pointed at the fat-bellied armchair.
So Winnie told the fat-bellied armchair,
'Chair, dance a cha cha cha!'

The stumpy little legs of the fat-bellied
armchair tried to dance, but it wasn't good.

39

'Meee hee heeeow!' laughed Wilbur.
And suddenly there was a rumble
grumble from all the furniture. The
fat-bellied chair growled.

'Ooo, look!' said Winnie. The fat-
bellied armchair was turning purple. It
was puffing up and stamping its little legs
and waving its fat little arms. Then it ran
towards Wilbur.

'Hissss!' went Wilbur, then he was off
and running too. Wilbur scrabbled up the
dresser, and behind curtains that tried to
wrap and trap him. Wilbur leapt onto the
table, his claws skidding and screeching
across the polished top, and—uh-oh!—
the table flipped onto its back and grabbed
Wilbur with all its legs as if it was a spider
and Wilbur was a fly.

'Mrrrow!' wailed Wilbur.

'Ooo, Wilbur, the furniture is cross with
you for all that scratching!' said Winnie.

But the furniture was cross with Winnie
too. The fat-bellied chair came up fast
behind the back of her legs, making her sit
down in it very suddenly. The chair
wrapped its fat padded arms around
Winnie's waist.

'Ooo, help! Dining chairs, help me!'
shouted Winnie. But those chairs all just
crossed their arms. 'Cupboard?' said
Winnie. The cupboard turned its back.
'Oh, pleeeeaase!' wailed Winnie. 'I promise
I won't make you do anything you don't
want to ever again!'

The fat-bellied chair let her go.

'Phew!'

The table let Wilbur free.

'Meeeow!'

But the stool marched over to the front door and opened it, **Crreeeeaaaakk!** Then the television, the bath, the bed, the chairs, the table, the hatstand, cupboards, and everything marched out of the door and away.

'They've left home!' wailed Winnie.

Winnie and Wilbur sat on the floor and ate their supper with fingers and paws because the cutlery in the dresser drawer had all gone with the dresser.

'We'll have to sleep on the floor with the cockroaches and ants,' said Winnie. 'It could be a tickly night!'

44

The floor was hard. The floor was
draughty. The creepy crawlies did tickle.

Sigh! **Squirm.** 'Ouch!' **Hump.**

'Meeow!' **Scratch-itch!** Sigh!

Neither Winnie nor Wilbur could get to
sleep.

'You know,' said Winnie, 'I liked our
old furniture just the way it's always been.
Oh, silly me!'

Then, suddenly, there was a **bang-bang-bang!** from the front door. **'Wiiinnniiieeee!'** yelled the dooryell.

'Ouch! Eeek!' Winnie got stiffly to her feet and walked stiffly to the door. 'I feel as if I'm made of blooming wood myself!' moaned Winnie.

Creeeeeak! She pulled the door
open. And in marched Winnie's bed, her
television, her table, her chairs, her bath . . .

'Hooo-blooming-ray!' said Winnie,
clapping her hands. 'Welcome home! Ooo,
here's my lovely favourite fat-bellied chair!'

'Hiss!' Wilbur leapt onto the windowsill.

'What brought you home, my furniture
friends?' asked Winnie.

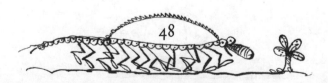

The hatstand pointed outside. It was stormy and wet and cold and dark out there.

'Not nice,' agreed Winnie. 'Well, you all settle just wherever you want to be, and I'll magic you back to being your proper selves.

'Aaah!' sighed the furniture, each piece happily setting itself down. Some things ended up in rather odd places.

'Abracadabra!' went Winnie. And
everything went quiet.

'Meeeow?' asked Wilbur.

'Yes, it's safe to come down now,' said
Winnie. 'And we can go to bed in a proper
bed, even if that bed is in the kitchen. Oh,
blooming heck! Even if the bed is wet!
And rumpled! And full of leaves! Ouch!
And has a blooming hedgehog family
nesting in it!'

But Wilbur found something much
softer and drier and warmer to sleep on.
It was Winnie's stomach. He slumped to
saggy sleep with a smile. Then he worked
his claws as he purred.

'Ouch! Now I know how furniture
feels!' said Winnie. 'Put those blooming
claws away, Wilbur!'

Which is
WITCH?

Winnie was doing some shopping. She told the shopkeeper, 'I'd like six big gob sloppers please, and a sugar mouse for Wilbur.'

'That cat isn't allowed in this shop,' said the shopkeeper.

'What?' said Winnie. 'Why not? Wilbur goes everywhere with me.'

'He's not hygienic, that's why,' said the shopkeeper. 'Look at those paw prints!'

'Oo, I can soon sort that,' said Winnie.

53

'*Abracadabra!*'

'*Uh!*' gasped all the other customers, because Wilbur was suddenly floating just above the ground.

A man in a suit pointed at Winnie. 'Sh-she's a witch!' he said, and he ran out of the shop.

'Now look what you've done!' said the shopkeeper. 'You've lost me a customer!'

'Only one silly man,' said Winnie. 'Everyone in the village already knows that I'm a witch.'

'I don't want you or your cat in my shop again!' said the shopkeeper. 'I can't be doing with complications! I just want normal customers.'

'That's not fair!' said Winnie.

'Out!' said the shopkeeper.

Winnie and Wilbur pressed their faces up to the shop window to see all the things they couldn't buy because they weren't normal.

'The trouble is,' said Winnie, 'I don't know how to be *not a witch.*'

'Meeow,' agreed Wilbur.

'But maybe,' said Winnie, suddenly grinning as wide as a banana. 'Maybe we could learn how to be normal!'

'Meeow?'

'What we need is a normal person to come and stay at our house. Then we can study them and copy what they do.'

Winnie chose a dusty musty damp empty room for a normal person to live in. She waved her wand. 'Abradacabra!'

57

Instantly, there was a plump soft bed, nice spider-web curtains, and a vase of nettles on a bedside table. 'Lovely!' said Winnie.

'Purrr!' went Wilbur.

'Good. Now, can you make a sign, Wilbur?'

Wilbur dipped a claw into some paint, and he carefully wrote:

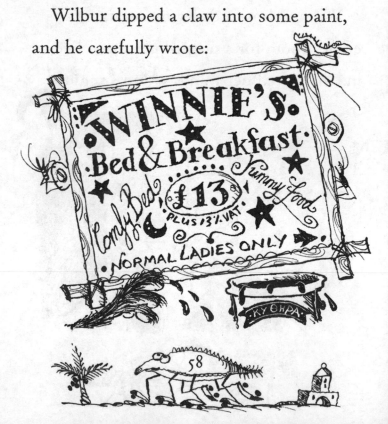

·WINNIE'S·
·Bed & Breakfast·
Comfy Bed £13 Yummy food
PLUS 13% VAT
·NORMAL LADIES ONLY·

They stuck the sign in place. Then they
waited. And waited.

'Do you think it's the price that's
putting them off?' asked Winnie.
So Wilbur wrote 'FREE' in
big letters over the sign.

Then they waited again, and waited
some more. 'Perhaps they've all heard that
I'm a witch, and they don't like witches?'
said Winnie.

'**Brriiiinnngg! Wiiiinnniiieee!**'
went the dooryell.

'Hooray! Somebody's come!' shouted
Winnie.

Crreeeaaaak! Winnie opened the door.
There stood a serious looking lady. 'I've come
for bed and breakfast,' said the lady.

'Oh, goody!' said Winnie. 'Er . . . excuse
me asking, but are you normal?'

'Yes, I think so!' said the lady.

'Brillaramaroodles!' said Winnie. 'What's
your name?'

'I am Dr Which,' said the lady.

'Really?!' said Winnie, clapping her hands
together. 'That's a funny thing because
I'm a . . . Ooo!' Winnie slapped a hand
over her mouth.

'That's quite all right,' said Dr Which. 'In fact you being a witch is the reason I am here. I am simply fascinated by witches. I intend to study you. You don't mind, do you?'

'That's as perfect as if baby slugs were born already coated in chocolate, that is! Because I want to study you too!'

'Well, that's marvellous,' said Dr Which.

'Oh,' said Dr Which when she saw the bedroom. She scribbled notes. 'Fascinating!' she said. 'Fascinating!'

'What is?' asked Winnie.

'Simply everything about you!' said Dr Which.

'Oh, dear,' said Winnie. 'Because I'm not fascinated by you yet.'

Winnie served a lovely alligator-egg soufflé for supper.

'How marvellously fascinating!' said Dr Which, and she made notes, but she didn't eat the soufflé. She spent the whole evening just looking at Winnie and looking at Winnie's house and looking at Wilbur. She scribbled lots of notes. 'Fascinating!' was all she said.

Normal people are a bit boring, was what Winnie thought. She went to bed early.

In the morning Dr Which asked, 'Winnie, is there a shop nearby? I'd like to buy myself some normal food.'

'Don't you like my food?' said Winnie. 'Oo, I know! Let's swap clothes and go to the shop that way!'

'Why?' asked Dr Which.

'So that you can feel what it's like being a witch,' said Winnie. 'And I can look normal and buy some gob sloppers.'

'What a marvellously fascinating idea!' said Dr Which.

Wilbur had to go with Dr Which. 'Mrrrow!' he complained.

'I'll get you lots of sugar mice!' promised Winnie.

Dr Which and Wilbur went into the shop. 'A normal cheese sandwich, please,' said Dr Which.

The shopkeeper held up a hand. 'Oh, no you don't!' he said. 'Out you go! You and your cat! No witches in here!'

'Fascinating!' said Dr Which.

'Out!' said the shopkeeper.

So out she went. And in came Winnie.

'Good morning, madam!' said the shopkeeper. 'And how may I help you?'

'You can give me a large bag of gob sloppers, that's how,' said Winnie. 'And a bag of sugar mice.'

'Gob sloppers? Sugar mice?' The shopkeeper peered closely at Winnie. Winnie glared back through Dr Which's glasses. 'Er . . . yes, at once,' he said.

As the shopkeeper was opening the jar
of sugar mice, Mrs Parmar came into the
shop with her shopping bag on wheels,
and **whoops!** one of the wheels caught
a box that shifted a display that toppled
onto a table that flipped like a seesaw to
shower fruit and vegetables everywhere.

Bop! Splat! Ping-ping! Boing!

'Ow, get off!' said the customers as they were pinged and splatted.

'You'll have to pay for cleaning this shirt, Mr Shopkeeper!'

'And for my black eye!'

'Oh, dear!' said Mrs Parmar.

'Oh, no!' said the shopkeeper. Mice came scurrying out of every nook and cranny, scrabbling for the food. It was CHAOS!

'Fetch our friend Winnie the Witch!'
said a customer. 'Her magic could save us!'

'Actually!' said Winnie, stepping
forward and taking off Dr Which's glasses.
'I am Winnie, Winnie the Witch.'
    'Hooray!'

'But I'm not allowed to do magic in the shop because it's not normal,' said Winnie.

Splat! Squeak! Mice were running up the shopkeeper's trouser legs.

'Oh, please do your magic, Winnie!' he pleaded.

So Winnie pulled out her wand. She waved it, '*Abracadabra!*'

Instantly everything jumped back into place . . . except for a couple of mice who sat and smirked at the shopkeeper.

'I d-d-don't like mice!' he said.

'Would you like a cat to catch them?' asked Winnie. 'Wilbur! In you come!'

Ting! Pounce! Squeak!

So Wilbur had normal mice as well as sugar mice for his tea.

74

WINNIE
on Patrol

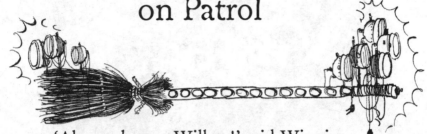

'Almost home, Wilbur!' said Winnie, steering her broomstick over the dusky wood.

'Twoooo!' called a cross owl.

Swerve! 'Whoops!' said Winnie.

'Meeeow!' Wilbur's fur was on end.

'You're right, Wilbur,' said Winnie. 'That owl should have lights! Let's fly up the village street. It'll be safer there.'

They swooped along the main road through the village, then, **Bang! Crash!**

Crunch! Tinkle! Winnie's broom hit
Mrs Parmar's bike. Bike, witch, cat, broom
and school secretary all fell **clatter-
crump!** into the road.

'Ouch, my bum!' said Winnie.

'Mrrrow!' went Wilbur.

'That's really dangerous!' said Mrs Parmar, standing up and wagging a finger at Winnie. 'What if I had been a lorry instead of a bike?'

'I didn't see you!' said Winnie.

Mrs Parmar put her hands on her hips. 'Where, Winnie the Witch, were your broom lights?'

'What lights?' said Winnie.

'Precisely!' said Mrs Parmar. 'You haven't got any! And everybody knows that a road user must have lights on their vehicle. It says so in the law.'

'Where are your lights, then?' asked Winnie.

'Here and here!' said Mrs Parmar, pointing. 'Oh. Er . . . the batteries seem to have run out. But at least I do have lights!'

77

They got safely onto the pavement, just
as a glare of bright lights came fast around
the corner.

Vrooom! The car whizzed past them.

'Coo-er,' said Winnie.

Gulp! went Mrs Parmar.

Wilbur's fur stood on end.

'We need to do something about this!'
said Winnie. *'Abracadabra!'*

Instantly, Winnie's broom and Mrs
Parmar's bike were strung with fairy
lights. Mrs Parmar had a flashing light on
her backside, and another two on the back
of each hand. Wilbur had a light on the
end of his tail. He thrashed it crossly. And
Winnie had a winking light on the top of
her hat.

78

'That's better!' said Winnie. 'Goodbye, Mrs Parmar.'

'Goodbye, Winnie. Ouch!' said Mrs Parmar as she tried to sit on her bike and found that a light wasn't a comfortable thing to sit on.

Back home, drinking mugs of cocoa, Winnie was frowning and stroking her chin.

'Hmmm,' she said.

'Meeow?' asked Wilbur.

'I'm just thinking about those little ordinaries,' said Winnie. 'In the winter it's dark by the time they come out of school. I think they all need flashing lights too . . .'

80

Brriiing-trrriiing-zzziiinngg!

went Winnie's telling-moan.

'Whoever . . .?' said Winnie. It was Mrs Parmar. 'Oh, yes?' said Winnie. 'I see . . . yes . . . you're quite right . . . well, yes . . . bye!'

'Meeow?' asked Wilbur.

'Guess what?' said Winnie. 'Mrs Parmar wants the little ordinaries to be safe too. She's asked me to be their Crossing Patrol Supervisor! With a uniform and everything! I'll look as smart as a jam tart!'

Next morning, Winnie and Wilbur reported to the school office.

'Is it a pretty uniform?' asked Winnie.

Mrs Parmar handed Winnie a great big long bright yellow coat, and a matching cap.

'They're a bit big!' said Winnie.

'Everybody will see you,' said Mrs Parmar. 'Now, here's the sign that you'll use to stop the cars.' She handed Winnie a big stick with stripes down it.

'Just like my tights!' said Winnie.

On one side it had a big red circle with a picture of children and on the other side there was a word.

'What does that say?' asked Winnie.

'It says "STOP",' said Mrs Parmar.

'Do you think they will?' said Winnie.

83

They went out to the road.

'What we really need is one of those black and white stripy things across the road,' said Mrs Parmar.

'Easy peasy!' said Winnie. She waved her wand. '*Abracadabra!*'

And there was a zebra running across the road.

Beeep! Screeech! Shout-shout!

'It doesn't work very well,' said Winnie.

'We don't want a zebra!' said Mrs Parmar, her chins all wobbling. 'Don't you know anything about the Highway Code?' she shouted as a noisy lorry rumbled past.

'Did you say a Highway Toad?' asked Winnie. 'I can get one of those. *Abracadabra!*'

And suddenly there was a toad in a motor car, buzzing back and forth through the traffic.

'No, no, no!' said Mrs Parmar. 'Dear, oh, dear!'

Vroom-beep-beep!

'I don't think your ideas are very good,
Mrs P,' said Winnie.

Mrs Parmar looked at Winnie. 'Just use
your lollipop,' she said.

Children were waiting to cross the road.
They told Winnie, 'Watch for a gap in the
traffic. Then hold up your lollipop and
walk into the road and the cars will stop.'

'Okey-dokey,' said Winnie. She waited for a gap. She held out her stick, and she stepped out into the road.

Vroom-stop! went the cars.

'Good cars,' said Winnie. She stood with her arms out like a scarecrow and the children all walked safely across the road.

'Brillaramaroodles!' said Winnie, and she stepped back onto the pavement. 'It worked! Easy-peasy squashed worm squeezy!'

'Well done!' said the children.

'Er ...' said Winnie, 'did you call my sign a lollipop?'

'Everyone calls them lollipops because that's what they look like!' said the children.

'Cooer!' said Winnie. 'It's a blooming big lollipop, isn't it?' Winnie stuck out her tongue. She gave her lollipop a great big lick. Then she made a face. **Spit!** **Euuggghh!** 'Horrible! Still, we can soon change that. *Abracadabra!*'

The STOP sign was instantly turned into shiny sticky sugary candy, raspberry flavoured in the red bits, lemon flavoured in the yellow bits, liquorice flavoured in the black bits.

'Mmmm, much nicer!' said Winnie.

The children jumped around her.

'Can I have a lick?'

'Please, Winnie, let me!'

But Mrs Parmar held up her hand

'Sharing lollipops is not hygienic!' she said.

'I'll give them a little lollipop each, then,' said Winnie. 'Everybody close your eyes and think of your favourite flavour. *Abracadabra!*'

Next moment, everyone had a lollipop. Even Mrs Parmar (her lollipop was flavoured with Brussels sprouts in gravy), even Wilbur (whose lollipop tasted of pilchards), even the car drivers.

'Mnn, that's all very well!' said Mrs Parmar, trying to sound cross but not being able to resist just one lick, and then another. 'But how am I going to get these children into school while you are offering them sweets out here?' Lick!

'Oh, sorry!' said Winnie. 'How about if ...*Abracadabra!*'

93

Suddenly the school was made of
gingerbread walls, with barley sugar door
handles and chocolate biscuit roof slates.

'Wow!' said the children, and they all
rushed towards school faster than they
ever had before.

'Er ... thank you, Winnie. I think,'
said Mrs Parmar, and she followed the
children inside.

'They'll need us again at going-home time,' said Winnie to Wilbur. 'It'll be dark then. I think I'll give all the little ordinaries bells to wear so that everyone hears them coming. And lights so we can see them. Perhaps smells too?'

Winnie and Wilbur trotted home on the zebra, sucking lollipops and thinking up lots more safety ideas. The toad drove off on his own adventures.

Enjoy more magic moments with
Winnie AND Wilbur